THE GLORY WHOLE REDEMPTION

THE CURSED MATCHMAKER
BOOK 3

SABRINA CROSS

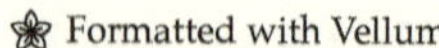 Formatted with Vellum

To Cassie Durand,
I'm not sure what it says about me that you heard
"Sentient Glory Hole" and immediately thought of me,
but writing this has been a blast.

AUTHOR'S NOTE

This is a sentient object romance. Humans will be getting it on with sentient objects. Don't worry, everyone is consenting.

If you read the last three sentences and think that's not for you, that's okay. There is still time to put this book down and walk away. No one will blame you. It's the sane thing to do.

But if you're going to stick around please be aware of the following:

Edging and denial, forced orgasms, bondage, mentions of past cheating, pegging, vaginal and oral sex.

If you feel I am missing anything please reach out to me at authorsabrinacross@gmail.com and let me know. A complete list can be found at www.sabrinacross.com

CHAPTER 1
JOSH

Life is all about moments. Moments of triumph and excitement. Moments of despair and grief. Moments of love. And moments of heartbreak.

All these little moments tie together to create the timeline of our lives. Except sometimes, one moment is all it takes to end life as you know it.

In one stupid moment, I threw away everything that mattered in my life. And now I'm being punished for it. Oh, I bet I know where you think this is headed. No, this isn't some sob story about a drunk driver going to jail or some other cable network feel-good movie nonsense about someone learning a lesson about what's really important in life.

Oh no. This is much more complicated than that. And much, much more fucked up.

My name is Joshua Gay, and two years ago, my girlfriend cursed me into a glory hole.

Now, I know what you're thinking. How did she curse you into a glory hole? What the fuck are you talking about? Grab the butterfly nets and the special hug jackets because this one has clearly gone around the bend.

That's totally valid. Two years ago, I would

have thought the exact same thing. Except now I am living it, and there's no denying that magic, real and terrifying magic, exists.

It's been two years of torment. But my curse appears to be weakening, and soon I'll be able to take my revenge.

I may have fucked up, but no one deserves to live as I have for the last two years. Now it's my turn to get vengeance.

And Bethany will never see me coming.

CHAPTER 2
BETHANY

"Have we figured out the electrical issue with glory hole booth five yet?" I glance up as the club owner Jason, my boss, walks into my office. I'm working on the schedule for next week and am happy for the distraction.

"I think so. It was working last night." Honestly, it has been working all along. But I've wanted to give poor Joshie a little break. For some reason, tormenting him isn't as much fun as it used to be.

I can't even work myself into a good mad about him revealing himself again. Oh, Olivia and Rob had been cagey about it, but I knew what they weren't saying. Something batshit crazy had happened in that glory hole booth, and they didn't know how to feel about it.

Thankfully for everyone involved, they'd been too anxious to get out of there to really focus on it. Goddess, I could practically smell the sex pheromones coming off of those two. It was almost as satisfying as seeing their auras merging together.

It is my favorite part of this job. Being able to identify perfect couples and manipulate situations until they get together. There is something truly satisfying in helping people find their perfect partner.

And if soulmate sex magic comes with a little extra oomph and gives me a power boost? Well, I won't complain.

"Good, let's get the schedule for it open." Jason continues to pepper me with questions about little issues that always arise when running a club of this magnitude. Thankfully, I'm able to give him answers for everything, and before long he's knocking his fist on my door jamb and is on his way.

Not that I really want to go back to scheduling staff and all of the other mundane tasks that come with managing a club. It's just that Jason is pure chaos energy, and it scrapes against my aura like discordant notes. Too long in his presence gives me a migraine.

I eye the schedule for the glory hole booths, the one currently missing booth 5. I don't want to open the booth.

I don't think too hard about why I'm hesitant to open it for the rest of the club. Especially not when I used it to my advantage last night. Thinking too hard about Josh creates a riot of emotion in me these days.

When I cast the vengeance spell, I was so sure that it was the right thing to do. I hadn't known what form it would take, only that it would bring Josh the torment I felt. But it has not brought the satisfaction I expected.

Oh sure, at first it was fun to torment him. To tease and use him. I enjoyed his discomfort and suffering. He earned it. His betrayal ripped me apart, and the pieces never went back together the way they were before.

But guilt was seeping in. And doubt.

I expected him to make excuses. I've been waiting for him to beg for forgiveness and mercy. But he never has. Not once in two years has he asked for my forgiveness or insisted on his innocence. Not once has he tried to ask for release.

The anniversary of the curse is coming up. It's been almost two years now, and I don't know how to feel. Parts of me are just as broken as I was the night he betrayed me. Parts of me have healed with jagged scars. And parts of me? Well, they're stupid and still in love with him.

CHAPTER 3
JOSH

'm off in some liminal space in my mind, dozing in the only escape I'm allowed. I don't sleep, not really. Not in the way humans are supposed to. I'm not allowed even that escape from my endless torment.

There's noise in the room beyond. I open my eyes, expecting to see the blackness that's been my constant companion for nearly two years, but I don't. Instead, I see a man in a pair of coveralls with a cleaning cart setting the room to rights.

I can see.

I don't understand what is happening, but something is clearly different. Between the return of sensation last night and now my vision, I know something is changing. I can feel it in my very soul.

The man sprays down the single chair with a cleaning solution before wiping it off. He pulls out the mop and begins cleaning the floor. I can hear music from his headphones. He bounces along to it as he works.

My foot taps along to the sound, and I freeze. I haven't been able to move my limbs in years. I wiggle my fingers, and they move too.

Sensation floods me as I push back against the

wall. It feels like I'm moving through a wall of bubble gum. It's sticky and pulls at me, trying to keep me trapped in its web but now that I can move, I'm not stopping.

I flex and stretch every part of me I can. I reach forward and push against the wall that has kept me prisoner for so long.

My body aches and I'm exhausted. I'm not sure how long I can keep fighting against the sticky, stretchy edges of my prison. Just before I give up, I fall free.

The floor is hard against my ass and back. My head strikes it with an echoing thump. I open my eyes and find myself looking up at the ceiling of my booth. The partition that had been a part of me for so long still standing.

I slowly sit up, enjoying the spinning in my head as I do so. Not because it's a particularly pleasant feeling, but because I can *feel* it. For so long I've been stuck in the numbness and blackness of my prison. Any sensation, good or bad, is a relief.

The janitor's music is loud, even on the other side of the partition. I need to figure out a plan. He'll be over on this side soon and how do I explain myself? I'm a six-three naked man sitting on the likely unsanitary floor of a glory hole booth in a high-class sex club.

I don't want anyone to find me before I find Bethany, but I also can't very well walk around the place with my ass out. I'm considering my options when the door on the other side of the booth opens. Fuck. Time's up.

But instead of the janitor leaving, someone else comes in. Someone whose voice I would know anywhere.

"Hey Kevin, I've got someone coming to double

check the electricity in here. Why don't you come back for the other half in a couple of hours."

"You got it, Bethany." I scramble to look through the hole just in time to see the janitor leave. Bethany stands in the middle of the booth watching him retreat. Once he's gone, she closes the door and looks at the wall.

She didn't lock it. Which is all the freedom I need.

CHAPTER 4
BETHANY

I wait until I'm certain Kevin is gone before I approach the partition and the glory hole where my ex-boyfriend resides. Everyone already thinks I'm strange, the last thing I need is for it to get out that I talk to glory holes.

Even if this particular one talks back.

"Your break is over, my love." I tell Josh, running my pointer finger around the edge of the hole. "The booth opens up again tonight. Do you think you're ready?"

There's no answer from Josh. I sigh and pull my hand away from the hole. I slam it against the wall to jolt him to attention before I reach into the hole for his cock. I freeze when I can't find it.

"Are you ready?" A low voice comes from behind me. I spin around, my hand still trapped in the hole, and there he is. The man I never expected to see again. He leans against the door with both arms propped on the top of the frame. His entire six-three body stretched and on display.

I'm immediately reminded of how good it had been between us. How he'd been able to do things to my body no one else had ever managed. And I hate myself for going there.

Sure, he knows how to play my body. But it is only because he spent so much time playing with other women's bodies. Even when he was supposed to be mine.

I pull my hand free of the hole and spin to face him head on. He gives me a dark smile as I prop my hands on my hips, instead of crossing them over my body like I want to. I will not take the defensive with him. Not after what he did to me.

"What's wrong, love?" He asks as he steps inside the room and closes the door behind him. "You look like you've seen a ghost."

Honestly, I would have been less shocked to have a ghost in the booth with me than Josh in the flesh.

Nope. Don't think about his flesh. His smooth, hot flesh. Don't think about what it feels like to have it pressed against me. Don't think about what it feels like to have him inside of me.

Stop it, Bethany! Get yourself together, woman.

From the dark glint in his eyes, Josh isn't here to make peace with the past. I am in danger. And I am not at all prepared for it.

"Just a little surprised to see you," I try to play it off as casual, even with my heartbeat ringing in my ears.

"I'll just bet you are." He takes a step forward, and I take a step back. But there's no space behind me, and my back ends up against the wall. My breath comes in pants as I watch him close the distance. I consider the size of the booth and the distance to the door.

I'm quick, but I'm also in three inch heels and a pencil skirt. It doesn't give me a lot of hope, but I've got to try. I wait until Josh is only a couple of feet away before I try to dart around him. He catches me with a hand around my throat and shoves me back against the wall.

"Uh-uh-uh, love. You're not getting away from me that fast." His hand isn't choking me, but my breathing is ragged all the same. The feel of his warm hand against my throat is too much after all this time. And when he steps closer and brings his body against mine, my legs go jelly.

"Did you think it'd be so easy? After all this time? After everything you've done to me? Did you really think I'd let you go?"

Words are stuck in my throat. I shake my head and attempt to keep eye contact even as I want to crawl out of my skin and escape this. I don't know what game he's playing, but I am in danger and every cell of my body knows it.

"Do you know how much hell you put me through in that hole? Do you know the agony of being on the edge for hours, days, and never being able to come?" His hand skims down my body to the belt tied at my waist, keeping my jacket closed and cinched tight. He tugs at one end until it comes loose, and I shudder under his hand.

His eyes are hot as they meet mine. He tugs the sides of my jacket open with his free hand, exposing my black lace bra beneath. He skims a finger down the center of my bra, where it rests between my breasts. The belt tickles across my stomach with the movement of his hands.

"You have no clue what kind of agony it was." In a move too quick to comprehend, he releases me and spins me around to press my face into the partition. My arms are wrenched behind my back and crossed over each other. He's wrapping the belt around them before I can even think to fight back.

"Let me go!" I growl out and try to pull my hands free. He moves too quickly, and I can't get them loose. "Haven't you learned I'm not someone to be fucked with yet? I can make what I did with the glory hole look like a day in the park."

"Not without your ritual you can't." He leans forward until the scruff of his stubble rubs against my cheek. "You think I haven't figured it out? That I haven't spent the last two years thinking it through? Oh baby, I've got your number."

I shudder at the heat of his breath in my ear as well as the words and the threat there. Because despite everything I've done to him and the rage in his eyes, I know one thing about Joshua Gay. And it is that he would never physically hurt me.

Whatever he has in mind, it isn't pain. And a sick, twisted part of me can't wait to find out what it is.

CHAPTER 5
JOSH

My cock feels like it's going to burst as I press my body against the lush curves of Bethany's body. The tip weeps cum and my whole body aches with need. Need to punish her. Need to drive myself into her and release two years of pent up tension. Need to make her feel exactly what I felt as I stood frozen in that partition.

It's the last need that wins out in the end. The need for revenge drives me hard as I finish tying off her belt around her arms and spin her around. I slam her back against the wall and take a moment to appreciate the fear in her eyes as she stares up at me. Especially because I can see the heat behind the fear. Oh, she's scared of what I might do. But she also wants it.

It's the combination of heat and fear that has me pushing forward, driving harder. I drop to my knees and use my grip on her hips to press her back against the partition. She wriggles, but she isn't going anywhere. Not until I'm ready for her to.

"Do you have any idea how painful it is to be on the edge for days at a time?" I slide my hands down her legs and then up again, dragging her tight little skirt up and out of the way. "Naughty little witch, not wearing any underwear while at work."

I shove her skirt up until it's over her hips and out of my way, leaving her completely bare from the waist down. She's wearing garters and stockings that perfectly frame her pretty little pussy. I trace my fingers over her smooth mound in a barely there touch that has her gasping. The sound is cut short as she bites it back.

Fuck no. Those sounds belong to me. I'm going to claim every last one of them. Every gasp. Every whimper. Every scream.

"Do you like knowing that anyone in the club could push your skirt up and fuck you? Do you like your musk scenting the air as you wander around watching all of the debauchery? Were you hoping for someone specific to reach under that tease of a skirt and touch you?" I spread my hands over her hips, holding her in place as I lean forward to breathe in her scent.

"No," she whimpers, and I know it's a lie. Bethany is a highly sexual woman and always has been. She is adventurous and likes to push the boundaries of decency. We've nearly gotten caught in compromising positions more than once.

"Liar." I slap her pussy, making her cry out. I follow it up by soothing my fingertips over her stinging lips and mound. My touch is gentle and light as I drag my fingers over her again and again. Teasing touches meant to make her squirm. And squirm she does.

"Tell me no, Bethany. Tell me to stop." I haven't gone too far yet. I haven't crossed the line. She can stop me with a word, and she knows it.

"Josh, please." She squirms in my grasp, and thrusts her hips to meet my touch. It's what I've been waiting for.

I lean forward and run my tongue over her seam. Not deep enough to split it apart and bare the warm, damp flesh beneath. Just enough to tease. I use my grip on her hips to hold her completely still as I lap her over and over again.

"Please, please. I need more." She's practically shaking in my hands as I continue my slow assault on her pussy. I press deeper, teasing her clit with wide, gentle strokes. It's enough to drive her higher, but not nearly the pressure I know she needs to get there.

I'm in Heaven and Hell. My cock drips precum as I devour the woman before me. The woman I loved more than I thought possible. The woman who made my last two years a living hell. Her taste is so familiar it felt like coming home. But I can't forget what she did.

CHAPTER 6
BETHANY

Josh's mouth is Heaven and Hell. He's always known my body in ways no one else has come close to. Having him there was a dream come true. His teasing touches and tentative strokes are torment.

I am shaking, my hands grasping at the wall and my own flesh for purchase as pleasure builds inside of me. His tongue gives me just enough pressure to send me spiraling but not enough to go over the edge. And his hands are stubbornly remaining on my hips in a powerful grip that is certain to leave marks.

He knows damn well I need something inside of me to come. He knows I can't come from clit stimulation alone. After what feels like eternity, I realize that's his game.

He's not going to let me come. He's not looking for my pleasure. He's looking for my pain. The point is driven home when my legs begin to shake as I beg for more and he stops.

The bastard stops.

And then he laughs. I hate him. More than I ever have before.

"Come now, love. You didn't think it would be that easy, now did you? Why would I want to give you the release you denied me? For years, you denied me. You're lucky I don't have years to punish you. To make you pay for what you did to me."

"Bastard." The word is breathier than I want, but my breath is caught in my chest as he laps away at my clit with teasing strokes.

Over and over again, he takes me to the edge only to stop. At some point, he drags me to the floor and spreads me wide. It's not until I'm panting and begging with my entire body shaking on the edge that he finally slides a finger deep inside of me and presses on my g-spot.

That's all it takes. I come with a scream. I bite my lip to suppress the sound.

"That's a good girl." Josh slides his fingers out of me and brings them to my mouth. I don't even think. I open and allow him to press them inside. "But I think we can do better."

I barely have time to process the words before he pulls his fingers free from my mouth and moves them back to my pussy. He presses two fingers inside me this time. The pressure is almost too much. I'm still tight from my orgasm and so sensitive.

"No, please." I try to wriggle away from him, but he puts his hand on my belly and pushes me down to the ground to hold me in place.

"Please? Of course. I'll give you all of the orgasms you denied me the last two years." His head dips and takes my clit into his mouth. I arch into him.

My arms ache, and my hands are going numb. I can't focus on that discomfort for more than a moment before I'm bowing up and into his mouth. My legs scramble on the floor as I try to find purchase as he fucks his fingers into me and sucks on my bud.

"Josh, I can't."

"Yes, you fucking can."

CHAPTER 7
JOSH

ignore the damp spot beneath my aching cock as I grind into the floor. I ignore the discomfort of my stomach, begging for food after two years in stasis. I ignore everything but the clench of Bethany's pussy and the taste of her coating my tongue.

She's come at least four times now and is barely able to do more than feebly try to wriggle away and twitch beneath me. I revel in her pleasure.

"Can't. Can't come again." Bethany pants above me. I curl my fingers inside of her and pulse on her pleasure point at the same time I begin circling my thumb over her clit.

"What are you talking about? You can absolutely come again." Within moments, her cunt is fluttering around my fingers.

"See, you little liar. You're perfectly able to come again." I grin up at her from between her legs. "You know what happens to liars?"

She whines and uses her legs to kick at me. Given the number of times she's come in the last hour, I'm pretty sure they're jelly. But I love the show of spirit.

"Liars get punished."

"Josh, no. I can't. I can't keep doing this. Please. I'm sorry."

"Sorry for what?"

"Everything. All of it. I'm so sorry. Just please, enough." Tears are running down her beautiful face. Her eyes are slits as she tries to find the energy to look down at me. She's beautiful. Perfect.

"Not enough." I say, surging up to my knees and pulling her across the floor to me until I can rub my weeping cock through her cum-soaked pussy. "It'll never be enough."

"Josh!" She cries out as I notch my head at her opening. "Please."

"One more. Give me one more, love." And I drive deep with one hard thrust.

Bethany screams out at the invasion of my cock. I freeze as the clasping heat of her body wraps around me. For the first time in two years, I'm inside a woman with full sensation. It's overwhelming, and if I can't get control of myself; I'm going to come before I get the orgasm I want out of her.

"Fuck, you feel even better than I remember." I give a shallow thrust into her and my eyes roll. Fuck, I'd forgotten how amazing it feels to be inside a woman.

"I can't." Bethany sobs. But she arches up into my shallow thrusts. Her legs around my waist, holding me close.

"Feels like you can." I reach down and rub my thumb against her swollen, red clit. I really have pushed her too far, but I'm a greedy bastard. I want to feel her come around my cock. I want to feel her pussy milk me.

"Josh!" A whine. A plea. A prayer.

She clenches around me, and I snap. I thrust into her hard enough to drive her up the floor toward the wall. She cries out and I pound into her, over and over again. Chasing the pleasure I've been denied for so long.

"Come for me," I demand, and press down on her lower stomach with one hand. I circle her clit with my thumb. "Now, Bethany. You owe me this."

Bethany comes on a keening wail. A sound so loud I'm amazed they can't hear it outside of the booth despite the soundproofing. It's all it takes. The first spasms of her cunt send me spiraling over the edge. Lightning shoots down my spine and through my balls as my cock begins to spurt.

My orgasm lasts forever. I come so hard my back bows. Cum quickly overflows Bethany's swollen pussy and leaks out between us.

"Fuck!" I roar, moving slowly as I drag out my orgasm.

"Enough. Please, Josh. I can't." Bethany sobs.

"Yes," I slide free and watch as my cum leaks free from her. "I've had enough."

CHAPTER 8
BETHANY

am still insensible when Josh slides behind me and helps me sit up against him. His hands are gentle as they unbind the belt from around my arms. He rubs up and down as blood flows back into the limbs.

"That's it, love." He helps me slide my aching arms back into my jacket and wraps the belt around me. The knot is sloppy and uneven, but it does the job of keeping my jacket closed.

"This doesn't change anything." My voice is raspy and sore. My mouth is as dry as a desert.

"It changes everything." Josh pulls me onto his lap, and my head lolls onto his shoulder. His arms wrap around me, and he holds me close. His fingers comb through my knotted mess of hair, carefully smoothing out the tangles.

"Will they notice you're missing?" His voice is low and vibrates through me.

"They've already noticed." The club wouldn't be busy for hours yet, but I never disappear during the day. Someone will have noticed. Josh doesn't say anything. He just hums and continues to work the tangles from my hair.

It's something he would have done in the past.

One of the things I always loved about him. Josh took aftercare seriously, and I was never left feeling alone or unappreciated. Nothing we've ever done in the past compares to what he just did to me.

"How?" I ask. The word is rough, and I wish for a glass of water. But Josh understands.

"I don't know. One minute I was in the wall and the next moment I was able to pull myself out. I guess your curse ran out of juice." His words are bitter but not harsh. And he doesn't stop his soothing movements in my hair.

It's not possible. The curse I used two years ago was a vengeance curse directly to the goddess of love herself. It was meant to be as cruel as the betrayal Josh had done. There should have been no end to it. Just as there was no end to my pain.

Except, the pain had ended. It had faded slowly over the years. Hadn't I just felt bad for him that morning? Was that moment of weakness enough to end the curse?

"I'm sorry." His words are soft. So soft, I'm not sure I heard him right at first. Except they're words I've craved for years. Words I would have given anything for two years ago. Words I never expected and never intended to entertain.

I steel myself against them now. It's not the time or place to have this conversation. Not when the doors open soon and I'm expected to do my job. Not here, where I've spent years tormenting him.

"Not now." I push away from him and wrap my hair up into a knot on the top of my head that I secure with a decorative hair band I wear around my wrist. I adjust my jacket to properly cover my breasts and move to the door.

"Wait here, I'll be back with some clothes."

CHAPTER 9
JOSH

half expect her not to return. I pushed her too hard, took things too far. Sitting in the spindly chair in the booth, I know this. But there had been no stopping after I got my hands on her.

Thinking with my cock was how I'd gotten into this mess in the first place. I knew better than to do it. But after two years of frustration, I hadn't been able to stop myself. It had been stupid and selfish.

"They're not going to be a great fit, but they'll work." Bethany says as she walks back into the booth carrying a stack of clothing and a pair of flip-flops.

"Thanks." I take the clothes and pull them on. The sweatpants are a size too small and don't quite meet my ankles. The t-shirt is a second skin, and I kind of worry about it coming apart at the seams. The flip-flops, at least, fit just fine.

"What now?" I ask as I smooth the shirt over my stomach. Which picks that moment to grumble loudly. "Sorry."

"I told them I'm leaving early. Let's get some food and we can talk." Bethany doesn't wait for me to respond. She just spins around and leaves the booth. I give the partition one last look and follow her out of the booth. I hope I never see it again.

———

"Thanks," I tell the waitress at the all-day breakfast diner Bethany takes me to. I lean back so she can put the plates heaping with pancakes, sausage, bacon, and eggs in front of me. Bethany assures the waitress she's still good with just coffee and water, and the woman gives me a smile before taking off for another table.

"What first?" I ask Bethany as I pour syrup over my pancakes and dive in.

"What happened?" She doesn't need to elaborate. There's only one thing she could be talking about.

"I don't know." I hold up a hand when she glares at me. "I honestly don't remember. I went to Erick's house. There were a lot of girls, a lot of booze, and it's all a blur. The last thing I remember was stumbling up the stairs to the spare room, alone. I was drunk, I was pissed, and I just wanted to sleep it off. I don't even remember seeing that girl there that night. The next thing I remember is waking up to you coming in."

Both of us are quiet, and I know she's going back to that last morning too. The morning Bethany had found me in bed with another woman. I'd been in nothing but my shorts, and she'd been wearing my shirt. I've had two years to think about that day, and I don't remember fucking the girl. But I have never been able to come to another conclusion.

Sure, Bethany kicked me out of her apartment. She told me she was tired of dealing with me and my shit. Which is how I ended up at Erick's house.

We were too old to be having a house party. We were too old to be getting blackout drunk. And Bethany had been right about me.

I was a loser. I had a job that paid the bills but didn't fulfill me, and I had no plans to find anything better. I spent most of my free time playing video games with the guys and not paying attention to the amazing woman who saw something in me worth loving.

Bethany deserves better than me. She always has. And two years ago, I was too fucking stupid to see it.

"Did you ever figure out who she was?" A part of me worried about what Bethany did to her. The rest of me hated her for ruining my life.

"No. I never bothered to try." Shock gave way to understanding pretty quickly. The girl didn't matter. She never mattered. Not really.

"What now?" I set the fork down, my meal mostly uneaten. My stomachchurning as I wait for her verdict.

"Nothing's changed." Her voice is cold, but her eyes are bright.

"Bullshit."

"I can't do this." Bethany drops a handful of bills on the table and starts to walk away. I grab her wrist in a loose hold.

"Bethany," It's a plea and a prayer. For nearly three years she's been the center of my world, and I'm not sure how to exist without her.

"Josh, no. Nothing has changed. You're still the guy who fucked someone else. And I'm still the girl who won't be cheated on."

"I'm the guy who took everything you threw at him for years. Haven't I been punished enough? Haven't I earned a second chance?"

I am probably insane for wanting another chance with the woman who literally turned me into a glory hole, but Bethany is the only woman I've ever loved. Even after everything we've done to each other and we've been through, she's the only person I can picture a future with.

CHAPTER 10
BETHANY

My heart screams against the idea of giving him a second chance to hurt me. I gave him everything, and it had taken one fight for him to throw almost a year of our lives away. How can I ever trust he won't do it again?

"I can't." I tell him. "How could I ever trust you again?"

Josh releases me and shoves to his feet. He looms over me as he runs a rough hand through his shaggy blond hair. Physically, Josh hasn't changed a bit since the day I cursed him. He's still tall, still broad, still built. His hair is the same too-long blond, and his eyes are the same golden hazel. And while I've started getting crows feet, his face is still as smooth as ever. I kind of hate him for it.

"I could have outed you for what you are any time in the last two years. I didn't have to keep my silence as you allowed others to use me day in and day out. I deserved every single moment of it for what I did to you."

"You sure as fuck didn't keep silent yesterday. Or with Samantha. How do I know you didn't talk to every single person who came in there?" Olivia told me there was something off about the booth.

She had been cagey about it, but I knew what had happened. Josh had talked again.

"Last night wasn't my fault. The curse changed and it was the first time my cock has been stroked in two years. It was reflex. And you said you weren't mad about that other couple."

He looks around and back at me. It isn't until then that I notice how much attention we're getting. I smile at the waitress, who is hovering nearby, and grab Josh's arm. I pull him behind me out of the restaurant and back to my car.

Neither of us say a word until we're closed inside. I grip the steering wheel with both hands and stare ahead. The car isn't on, and I didn't know where to go even if it was.

"Bethany, I'm sorry. Is that what you need to hear? That I'm sorry. Because I have never regretted anything more in my life. And not just because it led to me spending two years as a glory hole. It's because it hurt you. I hurt you. And that is the last thing I ever wanted to do."

I don't look at him. I don't want to see his face and know he's being sincere or if he's playing me. I don't want him to be sincere. I want him to be the villain he's been this whole time. I want to continue to hate him.

Because the alternative is forgiving him, and I'm not sure I'm ready to do that.

CHAPTER 11
JOSH

n the end, Bethany takes me back to her house and lets me sleep on the couch. My apartment, along with everything in it, is long gone. Bethany has my laptop, phone, and a couple changes of clothes I left at her place. All of my worldly belongings in one large box.

A part of me feels like I should be angry, but I'm not. I'm too tired. I just want to sleep, really sleep, and I can figure out my life tomorrow. Or try to gather the remains of it.

Bethany left me with a pillow and a blanket before closing herself in her bedroom. The couch is too short for me, but it'll have to do until I can figure something else out. I think about all of the people in my life and how they have no clue where I've been.

How do I explain my two year absence to them? Did Bethany tell them lies to cover my disappearance? Did they think I was missing? Did anyone even miss me?

Thoughts spiral through my mind as I think about the reality of my curse and how I disappeared from the face of the Earth without notice. My parents and I aren't close, and I hadn't been home in years even before I was cursed. Surely, they missed me.

I toss and turn, trying to sleep. I'm unable to stop my racing mind. There are just so many things that I need to know. Things I need to sort out. Things left unsaid.

At three, I give up. I climb off the sofa and head to Bethany's room. She owes me explanations, and I'm not waiting until morning. I can't stand not knowing anymore.

I ignore the closed door and walk in, intent on waking her up. But I don't need to. She's sitting in bed with her phone. Her long, dark hair cascades over her shoulders and conceals most of her breasts in the low tank top she's wearing.

Bethany looks up when I come in, and I can see the exhaustion in her eyes. She clearly is doing as well as me at the sleep thing tonight.

"Ever heard of knocking?" Bethany snaps, setting her phone in her lap.

"Where does everyone think I am?" I ask, completely ignoring her question. "I've been gone for two years, trapped in that booth. But I'm not a missing person. You're not suspected of my murder or kidnapping. No one seems to care that I disappeared."

I spent a lot of time searching myself and reading through socials before I came to find Bethany. Friends getting married, having babies, changing jobs, getting divorced. Everyone has gone on with their lives like my disappearance means nothing to them.

"They forgot." Bethany sighs and leans back against the headboard. I take my chance and sit on the foot of the bed. She doesn't tell me to get off, so I take the win. "Object permanence is such a fragile thing. It was easy enough to manipulate their thoughts so they just forgot."

"You erased me from existence entirely?" My pulse sped up at the thought of never existing. Coming back to my life is going to be hard enough, but impossible if no one remembers I existed at all.

"No, everyone still has their memories of you. They know who Joshua Gay is and they are friends with him. They just never think about you. Out of sight, out of mind. And you're all the way out of their minds. I'm sure they occasionally have a thought to check up on you, but it passes before they follow through with it."

I let that sink in. All of my friends and family were so easily made to forget to care about me. I found it impossible to believe no one cared enough to check in with me in two years. But I didn't have a single DM after the curse was enacted. My phone was shut off, but they could have reached out via social media or email, and no one did.

"I see," is all I can think to say.

I'm not mad. Being mad won't change anything. It won't take back what I did. It won't keep me from spending two years being used as a sex toy.

"Can you undo it?" Am I always going to be a passing thought? A ghost in the lives of my friends?

"It should have broken with the curse." For a second, she looks sorry. Sorry that no one had reached out? Sorry for what she'd done? Sorry for our whole shitty situation.

"I see," I say again and get to my feet. "Try to get some sleep."

I go back to the couch knowing I will not be doing the same. I'm not sure I'll ever sleep again.

CHAPTER 12
BETHANY

I t's been three days since Josh broke the curse, and I'm still waiting for something to happen. Eventually, he's going to snap and get mad. He has to. This calm acceptance is unreasonable.

And okay, cursing your boyfriend for sleeping with another woman isn't exactly reasonable either, but I never said I was. Just that Josh isn't acting reasonable either. And it feels like waiting for the other shoe to drop.

I go to work, the gym, the grocery store and when I get home, there's Josh. He's been cleaning and cooking and doing his most to prove that he deserves a second chance, but I've been down this road before. The second I give in and forgive him, what's to stop him from going back to the guy he was before? What's to stop him from hurting me again?

Josh wasn't a great boyfriend. He was more invested in his bros and video games than he ever was in me. But I trusted him. I loved him. And he destroyed that for me. I haven't allowed myself to trust anyone else for two years.

How much of what he is showing me now is actual change and how much of it is just a ploy to get back on my good side? I can't tell. And I can't trust myself to figure out the answer. Because I want to believe he's changed. I want to believe he's the person I fell in love with.

But fool me once and all that.

"Is everything okay, Bethany?" Jason asks, coming into my office and shutting the door behind him. It's never a good thing when he closes himself in here. He's always so careful to keep things open and aboveboard with zero room for others to question motives or actions.

I can count on one hand the number of times he's closed himself in with me, and it is never good news. Usually, it means I am about to fire someone, but he doesn't have that look on his face.

"Fine, there was an issue with call ins yesterday, but we handled it." And Jason wouldn't have closed himself in with me about something as simple as short staffing.

"I saw that. It didn't seem to be a problem. You handled it, just like you always do." He drops into the chair across from mine and sprawls out. It's a casual look for someone who was never casual. "That's not what I'm worried about. You've been working here for, what, five years now?"

"About that, yes." I'd started as a waitress and worked my ass off to become a shift manager and eventually a general manager. I fight the urge to fidget, unsure of where he's going with this.

"In that time, you have never left early. You have never called off. Heck, I'm not sure you've ever even taken lunch in the last three years. Which is bullshit, and you should absolutely be taking your breaks, by the way."

"Of course." I won't and we both know it. "I don't understand where you're going with this."

"You left two hours into your shift Sunday night

and have just seemed off since then. I'm not going to pry into your personal life. You don't owe me that if you don't want to share. But it's not like you and I want to know if you're okay. And let you know that I'm here to help if you need it."

The offer is sincere. In addition to being a genuinely good human, Jason is happily married to the most gorgeous and wonderful woman I've ever met. They were the definition of relationship goals. What I'd hoped for with Josh, but he has never been able to live up to.

"I'm fine." I don't plan on telling him the rest, but it kind of spills out. "My ex-boyfriend came back into the picture recently and I don't know what to do about him. He's been through some stuff and it seems like he grew up and changed, but do people ever actually change?."

I cover my face with my hands, embarrassed that I just trauma dumped all over my boss. But he just waits patiently until I look back up at him before he responds.

"I did." He holds up a hand to pause my words. "I was the biggest fuck boy in college. Rosie was everything I ever wanted, but never believed I could have. I fucked up. A lot." He smiles a little to himself. "I'm not saying your man has changed. I'm just saying that change is possible with the right motivation."

Jason pushes to his feet and heads to the door. "I'll get out of your way. But Bethany? If he doesn't realize you're the right motivation, he's an idiot and doesn't deserve you."

Then he was gone, leaving me to my thoughts and fears.

CHAPTER 13
JOSH

'm a stubborn man, often thick-headed. Some have even called me stupid. But even I know when it's time to give up and move on. No matter how hard I fight, no matter what I'm willing to forgive and forget, Bethany is not willing to meet me where I'm at.

I've tried to show her I've changed. That I'm willing to put her first. I've tried to do my best to be the man she needs, but she doesn't see it. When she isn't ignoring me, she's watching me like she's waiting for me to do something. What, I'm not sure.

By the time she gets home that night, I'm ready to have it out one last time. To say goodbye and move on. I've filled a trash bag with my meager belongings. My parents are sending me a plane ticket to get me home. It's the last place I want to be but the only place I have to go.

I thought about just leaving, but I didn't want it to end that way. For all the ways we've hurt each other, I owe Bethany better than that. And she owes me a goodbye. I won't let her go without the closure I need.

She comes in the same way she has the last few

days, as quietly as possible, sneaking up the stairs. I catch her on the third one.

"How was work?" It's not what I want to say, but the space between us is endless, and politeness is all I have left.

"Fine," Bethany says, playing polite right along with me. So fucking polite.

I want to needle her. I want to poke and prod until she gets angry. I miss seeing her temper flare and fire in her eyes. The bland mask she's wearing is painful, knowing exactly what hides beneath.

"I'm going to bed," Bethany says.

At the same time I say, "I'm leaving."

She freezes mid-step and turns to look over the banister at me. I want her to ask, to care, to give me something. But she's still an empty slate. And it hurts to know I did this to her. I broke her and made her wary. As much as I want to stay and fight, I know it's time to go.

"I called my mom. I'm going to go home for a while until I can figure my life out. She's sending me a plane ticket and I'll leave tomorrow." I was able to contact the bank, and I have some money but not a lot. And no way to access my cards since they'd all expired, and obviously I didn't get the replacements.

"Oh," Bethany nods once and continues up the stairs without another word.

"You can't leave."

I struggle awake. The living room is still dim, and I'm tangled in the blankets on the couch where I fell asleep after endless hours of staring at the ceiling and wishing for everything to be different.

Bethany is sitting at my feet, on the arm of the

couch. She's wearing an old, oversized t-shirt I recognize as mine. Her hair is falling in a waterfall over one shoulder, and everything else is shrouded in shadow.

"I have no reason to stay." It's not remotely true, but it's all the honesty I can muster. If I had a shred of hope she'd change her mind, I'd tear the ticket to pieces.

I shift and sit up to lean against the other arm of the couch. I leave my legs on the cushions and under the blanket. Her eyes drop to my bare torso, and I try not to read too much into the movement. I know she likes my body. There has never been any doubt about that.

It's just everything else about me that is the problem. And a part of me doesn't blame her. I was kind of a shitty boyfriend. I never bothered to put her first. I didn't pay attention to the little things. I had a lot of time to think while I was stuck in that wall, and I realized that I had messed up. Not just the night of our fight when I'd gotten drunk, but every day before that.

But if she doesn't want to give me a chance to prove that I can do better, there's nothing more I can do.

"So once again, things get hard and you just walk away. It's the Josh way." Bethany throws her hands up into the air, and I just gape at her.

"What are you talking about? You have given me nothing. You clearly don't want me here and I'm not going to keep crashing on your couch and prevent you from moving on." It's my turn to throw my arms up. "Do you think I want this? That the last two years have been me living the dream? You put me through hell, Bethany. You tormented me and tortured me. And I didn't say a single fucking word about it. Because I deserved it. I hurt you in the worst ways possible and there's no taking that back. But I'm not going to sit here and grovel and beg for scraps of attention from someone who clearly cannot stand the sight of me."

"And you destroyed me!" Bethany yells. "It ripped my heart out to walk in on you with another woman."

I want to argue. I want to point out that I was unconscious with another woman and that I couldn't remember sleeping with her. But what is the point? I'd been in bed with her. She was wearing my shirt. No matter how much I want to believe I wasn't the type of person to cheat on someone I love, I honestly don't know. I'd never seen the woman before in my life, and it wasn't like I could call up my buddy two years later and ask what happened. Fuck, I didn't even know her name.

"I'm fucking sorry! Do you have any clue how sorry I am? How much I hate that I hurt you? But me being sorry isn't enough for you. I can't change it. I can't take it back. And I can't pay for my sins, no matter how much you try to make me. There is never going to be enough for you and I can't keep doing this. I can't keep watching you be miserable with me here. So I'm doing the only thing I can, I'm leaving."

"Maybe I just need time," Bethany starts, but I cut her off.

"Two years, Bethany! You had two fucking years of time. I thought with the curse breaking maybe you had forgiven me already but I don't think you can. And that's fine. That's okay." I shift upward and drop one leg to the floor. I want to move. To get up and pace, but my pants are on the floor and Bethany isn't looking away.

"I don't want to hurt you anymore, Bethany.

And me being here hurts you." I want so much to reach forward and touch her, but it feels like she's miles away. I can't imagine a world in which she would welcome my touch again. Even though it's the only thing I want.

"And you think leaving won't hurt me?" Her voice is quiet. I barely catch the words. My heart catches in my chest as they sink in. She can't mean it. I want to believe it so badly, but it hurts too much to get my hopes up.

"I think no matter what I do I'm going to hurt you. I think you're not ready to forgive me and you'll never be able to forget. We've done so much damage to each other over the last few years that there's no starting over and no moving forward."

Fuck it. I grab my pants from the floor and spin to slide them up my legs under the blanket. I'm wearing boxers, but they've seen better days and don't contain everything. I'm not trying to flash someone who can hardly stand the sight of me.

"I don't know how to trust you anymore," Bethany whispers.

This time, I can't stop myself. I leave my pants unzipped and unbuttoned and move to my knees before her on the couch and cup her cheek. Her skin is so soft, her hair silk against the back of my hand. I savor the warmth of her face in my palm and under my fingers as I tilt her head to look up at me.

"I know. I understand. And I don't blame you." I drop my forehead to press against hers and close my eyes for a moment. They fly open when Bethany hitches back a sob. "No, baby, don't cry. Please, don't cry over me."

The last thing I want is her tears. I wanted something to break the mask, but not this. Never this. I never wanted this strong, fiery woman to cry over me.

"I don't know how to trust you," she repeats. Her eyes open and look up into mine. Her hand comes up to brush over my lips, my cheek. "I also don't want to let you go."

CHAPTER 14
JOSH

t would be so easy to tell Bethany I'll stay. That I'll stay as long as she wants me. That I'm here, however she needs me. But it would break me to be here, knowing she isn't all in. I want to do that for her, but in the end, it would break both of us.

"It's all or nothing, Bethany." I tell her, pulling away and dropping my arms to my sides. I need to break contact before my resolve waivers. "I'm here. I'm all in. I can forgive everything you put me through but I can't be here if you're just waiting for me to fuck up again."

I push to my feet and turn away from her. My shirt is on the back of a chair, I snag it and pull it on. I have to get out of here. If I don't, I'll do something I regret. There's been enough hurt between us. I'd be a monster if I added to it.

"Goddamnit Josh, I can't promise that!" Bethany is up, moving toward me as I make my way to the door. She grabs my arm and spins me around to face her. I go willingly, eagerly. I want her to tell me what I need to hear. I want her to make me stay.

Which is why I need to leave.

"You know what it was like for me growing up. New boyfriends, cheating, drama. I had one rule, one fucking rule about our relationship, and you broke it. Trust doesn't come easily for me and you destroyed it. And over what? A fight about cleaning the fucking house and buying me flowers every now and then? That was enough to destroy almost a year of time together?"

"It's not like I planned it! I don't even fucking remember it!" I throw up my hands, throwing her grip off of me. "It wasn't some malicious fuck you, it was a drunken mistake I will regret forever. But what you did to me? You told me magic was all about intent. And that was some malicious fucking intent in that curse you cast on me. I can forgive you. You can't even try to forgive me."

Now my blood is boiling at the injustice of the situation. What she put me through was literal Hell. And I took all of it. Because I fucked up and I hurt her in the worst possible way. I knew that. But if I could find a way to get over it, so the fuck could she.

"I can't do this anymore, Bethany. I can't. I'm done." I turn back around and head to the door. I'll come back later for my meager belongings, before the uber gets there in the morning to take me to the airport. A walk will do me some good.

I reach for the door handle, and Bethany is there, forcing her way between my body and the door. I find myself flush against her, and my cock reacts. Stupid, fucking thing. It's nothing but trouble.

I've fucked my hand so many times in the last few days, trying to take the edge off. But after years of being on edge and unable to come, it's hard to let myself go. It was another thing Bethany had taken from me that I wonder if I'll ever get back.

"You need to let me go," I tell her, my hand still on the handle.

"I can't!" The words come out on a sob. "Do you think I haven't tried to stop caring so much? Do you think I want to feel this way?"

She slams a hand on her chest. I can see the tears falling down her cheeks. They carve ghostly paths down her face. It breaks my heart but I force myself to stand strong. I have to.

For both our sakes.

"If you can't forgive me, you have to learn how to forget me." I want to beg her for forgiveness. I want to make her want me as much as I want her. But I don't. I gently take her by the arms and move her aside. She takes one stumbling step, another. And then locks up and refuses to move out of my way.

"Stop." She slams her hands on my chest and fists them in my shirt. "Stop trying to leave me. Don't you understand? I'm trying! This is me trying!"

It's my turn to freeze up. I try to take in the words, the actions, to put it all together into something that makes sense. Wishful thinking has me wanting to break, to fall to my knees and hold her tight. I reach up and wrap my hands around her fists. I'm tall, but so is she, so it doesn't take much to bend down until our faces are together.

"Baby, I'm going to need you to be very clear what you mean right now."

"I mean I want you to stay. I'm not saying I can forgive everything. Not right now. But I'm saying I want to try. I want to try to get over this, to trust you, to make this work. I want this, you, us." She leans forward and buries her face in my chest. I can feel the dampness of her tears seep into the fabric, and they break my heart. I don't want her tears. I never have.

I release her hands and drive my fingers into the

silk of her hair and hold her to me. I breathe deep, taking in the woodsy scent of her shampoo that I always loved. My heart aches as I think about her words. Think about what this could mean for me, for us.

It's everything I want but don't quite believe. What if she decides she can't forgive me? How long do I give her? I've already lost two years of my life, how much longer can I stay in stasis waiting to move on?

Of fucking course, I'd rather we move forward together. But can I trust that she'll ever get there? She has spent the last few days avoiding me, and years tormenting me. Bethany got off on my pain, and that's not something I can forget either.

"Please Josh, stay." Her arms wrap around my torso and hold me tight to her. She clings in a way she never has before. And I break.

"Three months," I tell her. "Three months and we either move forward or we move on. I can't keep waiting for you."

"Okay, yes. Yes." She leans in and seals the deal with a kiss.

CHAPTER 15
EPILOGUE - THREE MONTHS LATER - BETHANY

"Fuck Bethany!" Josh exhales the words as I work my way into him. He's so tight around the bright pink silicone cock I'm wielding. I don't reply, just keep grinding into him, the base of the strap rubs against my clit in a delicious friction.

"Please, please," Josh pants, "Baby, we don't have time for slow. Just fuck me already."

He's right. We don't have time for slow. We have people arriving in less than an hour. But I'm selfish and don't want to rush this. Plus, I don't want to hurt Josh, and he's so tense.

"Relax baby, I'll take care of you." I glide my hands up the globes of his ass and out, spreading his cheeks wide. He and the strap are glistening with lube, but I reach for the bottle and trickle more over them both.

"Feels so good." He moans, pressing back against me.

Who knew that something we'd both considered his torment would turn into one of our favorite things? I'm a dominant woman by nature and have always been a switch in sexual situations, but I'd never considered pegging anyone until Josh was in the wall. And Josh was very much not the type of guy who considered taking anything in his ass before the curse.

Now? Neither of us could get enough. I love feeling him open for me. The way his body clenches down and around the cock of choice. There is power in it, yes. But there is also vulnerability. Something I don't allow myself enough of.

Josh makes it safe to be soft. To be hard. To be whatever it is I need to be. And he revels in it with me.

"Now!" Josh demands, and I obey. I thrust forward and sink home. We both cry out as my hips meet his ass and the base of the dildo presses against my clit.

"Oh, fuuuuck," I groan before pulling out and thrusting in again. I set a hard, fast rhythm. It's one we both love and that will get us both off quickly. I drop my arm around Josh's waist to wrap my hand around his cock. He's rock hard and leaking on the bed.

"Look at my good boy," I mutter in his neck. "You're taking my strap so well. Are you going to come for me?"

"Please, Bethany. Please." His hips jerk in sporadic movements against me before his entire body tenses. I squeeze his dick harder as he begins to spurt on his stomach and the towel we'd tossed on the bed.

"That's it, baby. Come for me." I grind deeper, pressing against the grinder on the back of the harness. Driving it into my clit. It's not enough. And Josh knows it.

In a flash, he's pushed me off of him and has reversed our positions until I'm under him. He helps me work the harness off over my hips in frantic movements and then here's there. Right where I need him.

His mouth presses against my cunt, licking and sucking. He drives two fingers into me. There's no resistance. I'm so wet and close. It only takes a few moments before I'm clenching around his hand. But he doesn't let up.

"You've got more for me," Josh says against my lower lips. He pulls his fingers out and presses them to my lips as he moves lower to lap at my clenching hole. I open for him, mouth and legs. I taste myself on his fingers while he devours me with long laps and probing thrusts. I drape my legs over his shoulders and allow him better access to my hole.

"More," I demand. It comes out a whining plea.

"Everything you need," Josh promises.

———

An hour later we're both out in the garden greeting guests as they arrive. It's a small gathering, just a mix of family and friends. We've left the garden gate open, and people are flowing in. The twinkle lights on the fence and canopy are on, giving everything a warm glow.

"Erick is here," I tell Josh, knowing he's anxious about seeing his oldest friend. They reconnected since the curse broke but haven't had a chance to actually meet up. Erick is married now, with a baby and another on the way.

"Why does this feel like meeting the parents all over again?" Josh asks, gripping my hand as we cross to the gate to greet him. There's a blond woman by his side. She's hugely pregnant, and her stomach is stretching the confines of her dress to the limits.

"Because he's your oldest friend but also a total stranger. And because you're still just a little pissed at him for not noticing your absence for two years?"

"It was a rhetorical question, love." Josh drops a kiss to the top of my head before releasing me to clasp Erick in a dude hug. I turn to the woman at Erick's side and freeze.

I know her. I would know her anywhere. My blood surges hot as I look at the woman who fucked my boyfriend.

CHAPTER 16
EPILOGUE - THREE MONTHS LATER - JOSH

can tell something is wrong the moment I step away from Erick's embrace. There's a chill coming off of Bethany that I don't understand.

She has reason enough to hate Erick, but she's been nothing but supportive of me rekindling that friendship. She was the one who invited him tonight.

"Never thought I 'd see the day Joshua Gay got engaged. Congrats man," Erick says, clapping me on the shoulder. "Married life ain't all bad. When you've found the right person."

He reaches out to wrap an arm around his wife, and that's when I really look at her for the first time. And oh, that face. That face is familiar. I'm still struggling to place it when Bethany gives a feral grin.

"Who's your wife, Erick?" She asks, slinging an arm around my waist. "And did you know she fucked my fiance?"

There's a moment of silence, and it clicks into place. The woman at the party. The one wearing my shirt. The one who destroyed my life.

She was Erick's wife.

Oh, she hadn't been back then. Erick hadn't

been dating anyone. He'd been chasing some red-head for months. But this was definitely the girl from the party.

Oh. Oh, shit.

The blond's eyes widen in shock, and she spins to look at Erick. "This is your friend? I should have put it together. I should have. Oh my god."

"Bridget?" Erick is more bewildered than upset. But I can see the uncertainty there. He looks from her to me to Bethany and back again.

"I didn't!" Bridget seems sure about it. She looks from Erick to me. "We didn't."

"So, you just climb into bed with naked men while wearing their clothing?" Bethany demands. I wrap an arm around her. It's not in comfort but an effort to keep her by my side. She's practically vi-brating with anger, and I know firsthand how ugly that can turn.

"Oh, my god. You don't remember?" Bridget brings a hand to her face and rubs between her eyes before dropping it to cradle her rounded belly. "Crap, is this why you guys had a falling out? Please tell me it's not."

"Not Erick and I, no." I say slowly, "But it was definitely an issue with Bethany."

"This is so embarrassing." Bridget lets out a breath and stares Bethany in the eye. She clearly doesn't see the danger she's in because she's per-fectly at ease when she blows our world apart.

"I never slept with Josh. I mean, I slept in the same bed as him. But we didn't sleep together, sleep together." Bethany's body goes completely rigid. "I was at the party with some friends and got totally trashed. And then the bitches abandoned me there!"

I remember the group of women. They'd been younger, too young to pay attention to. And I hadn't been there looking for a hookup. I'd been drinking away my fight with Bethany and contemplating the future breakup. I have no memory of Bridget specifically, though. Not before the morning we woke up to Bethany slamming into the bedroom.

"Anyway, Erick was…busy." She shoots him a glare, and he has the grace to look embarrassed. No need to guess what he was busy with. "And some dude had already passed out on the couch so I figured I'd take the spare room. But Josh was already there. I spun around to leave and ended up puking all over myself. Josh woke up long enough to throw me a clean shirt to change into and then passed back out."

She wasn't serious. She couldn't be. There was no fucking way the last two years of my life were stolen from me because I gave some drunk girl a shirt.

"I figured he was out and it beat sleeping on the floor so I climbed into bed with him. I tried to explain when you came in that morning but, gosh you were so mad." She looked to me, to Erick, and back. "You really don't remember?"

"Not a fucking thing." I tell her. I don't know how to process the information. I don't know why she would lie about it. She and Erick weren't together and he hooked up with someone else at the party, so it wasn't like she was trying to hide cheating on him. She seems pretty fucking sincere.

And if she is telling the truth…

"Oh, my goddess." Bethany looks at me, horror in her eyes. I feel it in my chest. There's a tightness as I think about everything we've done to each other. Everything we'd been through. And it was all for nothing.

"Excuse us," I say, tightening my arm around

Bethany and leading her away and into the garage where we can have a moment of privacy.

"Josh," The word is a broken whisper. "I didn't–"

"Neither of us did." I say, running my hands through my hair. "Holy fuck."

Bethany reaches for me but then drops her hand and steps away. She backs into her car and spins around to press her hands against the hood. Her breaths are coming in ragged pants, and her shoulders shake with the force of them.

"I'm sorry. I'm so sorry." She chants the words in a broken voice, and I can't take it anymore.

I cross the space between us and cage her between me and the vehicle. I slam my hands down on the hood on either side of her, keeping her in place.

"Listen to me," I say, pressing against her back. "It doesn't matter. None of it matters. This is what matters. Right here, right now. You and me."

"The things I did to you, I can't." She spins around in my arms and grasps the collar of my shirt. "Josh, that spell was never meant to be used like that. You were innocent. I jumped to conclusions and stole everything from you."

"Stop." I grab her hips and lift her onto the hood. I force my way forward until I stand between her legs. "You didn't know. I didn't know. Because I was so fucking drunk I couldn't remember a thing. We both assumed."

"How are you so calm about this?" She yells.

"I have everything I want. Right here, right now, I have the life I want. I don't give a fuck what it took to get me here. Would I have preferred to avoid two years as a fuck hole? You're goddamn right. But let's be for real here, I was an idiot and an asshole. If this hadn't happened, we wouldn't have lasted. I was too young and too stupid to see what was important and I would have lost you."

"You can't know that." This time it's a whisper. "You couldn't know that."

"Baby, don't lie to me. Or yourself. We fought all the time and I was a twenty-eight year old going to get blackout drunk at a buddy's house because I had a fight with my girlfriend. I wasn't growing up anytime soon. Maybe this needed to happen."

"I have to make it up to you. Goddess Josh, I can't…" She looks on the verge of tears again, and I need to stop them.

I know just how to distract her. I slide my hands up her thighs, pushing her skirt up with them. In a flash, I hook my fingers under her panties to slide them down her legs. "You're going to spend the rest of our lives making it up to me."

"Josh, we have people out there." She doesn't object when I press her thighs wide, though. Or when my hands fall to my belt buckle. "We can't."

"We can. We are." I free myself from my pants just enough to line up with her pussy. She's still damp from earlier as I slide the head of my cock through her folds. She arches up into me and I notch the head of my cock at her opening.

"Josh," Bethany clutches my shoulders and angles her hips until I'm able to thrust into her with one movement. "Fuck."

"Every day, Bethany. You're going to have lots of chances to make it up to me. For the rest of our lives." I move inside of her, slow and teasing. Sure, our friends, family, bosses, and coworkers are on the other side of the door. Yeah, we are being incredibly rude. But I don't give a fuck.

"Josh, yes, goddess." Bethany tries to move, but I grab her hips and keep her exactly how I want her. "I love you."

"I love you. So fucking much. You're mine, baby. However we got here, whatever it took, you're mine now. And I'm never letting you go."

I grip her harder and slam into her, taking my smooth, slow glide to something hard and brutal. The punishing fuck she needs. Later, I'll bend her over my lap and spank her ass for every single person who fucked me as a glory hole. Exact my revenge on her body with so much pleasure she'll forget her own name before I'm done.

But the truth of the matter is, she's mine. And it doesn't matter how we got here. It just matters that we spend the rest of our lives loving each other.

Though I may burn her spell book just in case.

I'm a forgiving man. But I'm not fucking stupid.

ABOUT THE AUTHOR

Sabrina Cross (she/her) is a neurospicy 80's baby from the middle of nowhere Michigan, where she still lives with her cat. She came into her monster romance era early when she fell in love with Beast from the 1997's X-Men animated series.

After discovering sentient object romance in early 2023, Sabrina decided to embrace what she calls her 'Hold My Beer' style of writing and gave into the lifelong dream of being an author. When not writing weird monster/sentient object smut, Sabrina can be found hanging out on social media (@authorsabrinacross), reading, or hoarding office supplies.

ALSO BY SABRINA CROSS

Yarn & Monsters Series

A True Love Spell Gone Wrong...

When four friends perform a true love spell, things go terribly wrong. Now they're locked into a deal with the devil and have only a year to find love and happiness or their souls are destined to face the flames. Armed with a demon guardian; Clover, Jasmine, Fern, and Violet are determined to beat the devil and save themselves. Except, this curse might be the best thing that's ever happened to them.

Corny: A F/F Candy Corn Romance

Snuggle: A M/F Demon Teddy Bear Romance

Tangled: A M/F Friends-To-Lovers Sentient Object Romance

Knotted: A M/F Demon Werewolf Romance

The Cursed Matchmaker Series

Never Piss off a witch. Or else you may find yourself trapped in a glory hole booth at an upscale sex club. But when the perfect couples hook up anonymously, Josh has no choice but to speak out and help them find love.

The Glory Whole Package

The Glory Whole Experiment

Retro Whimsy Series

Getting Railed

"Welcome to Retro Whimsy!"

I hadn't planned on buying anything when entering the new vintage store during my lunch break but somehow found myself leaving with a toy train set.

What could have been written off as an impulse purchase became so much more when those trains come to life.

Now I'm stuck dealing with the consequences of a god curse and deciding if I have what it takes to help break it.

Light Me Up

He was the first man to ever turn me on. When he flipped my switch and lit me up that first time, I knew he was it for me. There would never be another.

Pounded by the Pommel Horse

Elena loves being on top. When the elite gymnast is challenged to defeat her gym rival on the pommel horse, she's up for the task. But is she up for the ride when the pommel horse shapeshifts into a man? A very, very naked Man?

Christmas with the Monster

He's Got a Package for Her... Devynn expected her first holiday without her kids to be difficult. But nothing could have prepared her for what she found under the tree just after midnight.With the help of his magic sack, the furry, green giant promises Devynn all kinds of pleasure. But would one night with the Christmas monster ever be enough?

Sentient Pen15 from Outer Space

Liam had spent a lot of his childhood obsessed with the legends of the local mines. The abandoned tunnels underground had driven dozens of workers insane and young Liam was desperate to get to the bottom of it. But he found more than he bargained for down there.

Infected by parasitic space mold, Liam has held himself away from relationships for years. When things spark between him and the girl next door, he has no choice but to reveal the truth: his manly appendage is also the bane of his existence.